The Mystery at the Birdfeeder

A Photographic Adventure

To _____

From _____

Date _____

The Mystery at the Birdfeeder
A Photographic Adventure

By
Wayne L. Brillhart

Edited By
Cecilia A. Haslam
Monica Tombers
Elena Covalciuc

HMSI
Publishing L.L.C.

Plymouth, MI U.S.A.
www.PublishHMSI.com

The Mystery at the Birdfeeder
www.mysteryatthebirdfeeder.com

Published by HMSI Publishing L.L.C., a division of HMSI, inc.
www.publishHMSI.com

Authored by Wayne L. Brillhart

Copy Editing by Cecilia A. Haslam, Monica Tombers
Photo Editing and Cover Design by Elena Covalciuc

Publishing Coordinator: Jennelle Jones
Publisher: David R Haslam

Published by HMSI Publishing L.L.C.

For information about permissions to reproduce any part of this work, write to
Permissions,
HMSI Publishing L.L.C.
Suite 3b,
50768 Van Buren Drive,
Plymouth, MI 48170, U.S.A.

ISBN - 10: 0-9842662-2-4
ISBN - 13: 978-0-9842662-2-7

0050-0002

Printed in The Philippines

10 9 8 7 6 5 4 3 2 1
February 26th, 2010
10:30

To God who made the birds
and
Bird lovers everywhere

Hello! My name is Purdy.
In this family, it's my job to
look after the yard all
year long.

A special part of my job is to look after the birdfeeder. During the winter months, I like to watch it from the warmth of the big house.

We try to keep
the birdfeeder full of seed.
All different kinds of birds like
the seed. But one morning, there was
a mystery.

I looked out of the window and the birdfeeder was lying on the ground. It was not broken, but the seed was all gone. What happened?

I didn't see any birds or any animals.
I needed to find out what happened!

We filled the birdfeeder again and hung it in its place.
I sat on my dog house to see what I could find out.

I spotted Carl, the Cardinal,
up in his favorite tree.
"Can you help me solve the mystery
of the birdfeeder?" I asked.

"Sure. What happened?" Carl asked.
I explained as he flew down onto the birdfeeder.
Carl had no idea who did it. "I'll wait here and see who
arrives. Maybe someone can tell us." chirped Carl.

A slate-colored Dark-eyed Junco arrived on the other side, as Carl ate his breakfast.

"I'll move over here so the other birds can eat,
and I can talk to them," chirped Carl.
"Sounds good to me!" I barked back.

"Yum, this seed looks good!
I've never been here before,"
said the Junco.

While he ate, Nancy, a Red Breasted Nuthatch arrived.
"Hi, Carl. What's going on?" she said.
Carl explained the mystery to both of them.

"My name is Jimmy,"
interrupted the Junco.
"Maybe I can help you find clues."
"Thanks Jimmy. That would be
great!" tweeted Carl.

"I'll watch from this big tree," sang Jimmy.
He flew up to a branch high above my head.

Meanwhile, Nancy looked over the seed.
"Wow! There sure is a lot left," she called to Carl.

"I'll be back to snack later!!!!!" sang Nancy as she flew away.
"Well, she didn't eat much," Carl chirped to me.

Terry, the Tufted Titmouse, flew in and landed on the feeder. He was hungry for some brunch.

"Wow! What a selection! Thanks for refilling the birdfeeder, Purdy," he chirped quickly.

He picked the biggest, tastiest seed he could find and was gone in a flash.

Moments later, Will, the White Breasted Nuthatch, landed on top of the feeder "Look, the birdfeeder is back up!"

"Did you see who knocked it down?"
I barked. "No," replied Will.
"I just saw it on the ground."

"While I'm here I had better grab some lunch
and get a move on," Will continued. Soon he took
flight again and sang "I'll be back!"

Charlie, the Chickadee, flew in fast to see if there was enough for his lunch.

As he landed, he stretched his wings and asked "When was the birdfeeder picked up?"

Carl answered, "It was put back up this morning. Did you notice who knocked it down?" Charlie grabbed a bite and flew over to talk to Carl.

"I noticed it on the ground early this morning, but did not see who had done it." He decided to rest and watch to see what would happen next.

Later that afternoon, Nancy stopped by to see her friend Carl.
"Purdy and I are still trying to find who knocked the
birdfeeder down," Carl told Nancy.
"I have not found any clues either," chirped Nancy.
They shared some seed before she was on her way again.

A little later... "I'm back! Did you find anything out?" Will asked as he stopped by for his dinner. "Nothing yet," Carl tweeted, while I woofed in agreement.

Then Will flew off again.

Carl was nibbling his favorite seeds when another friendly face arrived.

It was his sister, Carol.
"Are you still eating lunch?"
she chirped in surprise.
"No, I'm helping Purdy investigate why
the birdfeeder was on the ground this
morning," he answered.
"Let's go fly around for some clues!"
chirped Carol and they flew away together.

Jimmy flew down from the tree.
He took over watching, for Carl.

Back in the tree, Ruby, the Red-bellied Woodpecker, showed up to see what was happening. "What's all the excitement?" she asked me, and I explained.

"I can help! I have a great view from up here, Purdy!"
"Thank you!" I barked. "Keep a sharp eye out, Ruby."

Suddenly, I heard a rustling from the woods. "Maybe this will solve the mystery," I thought. "What could it be?" Then I barked "Everyone watch carefully!"

Three Turkeys, led by Tammy, came out of the trees for their dinner. "We only eat the seeds on the ground, Purdy. Sorry we can not help you," she replied to my questions.

When they had finished eating, off they went.
"Gobble! Gobble! Goodbye, Purdy!" Tammy said.
"Good luck solving your mystery!"

"The Turkeys are sure big, but they did not touch the feeder."
I thought. "What could have knocked it down?"
Up in the tree, Ruby cried "Look! I see tracks!"

I looked carefully and could see that they were not Turkey tracks. They belonged to something much bigger. But what?

Another noise from the woods made me look up again!
In the distance was a deer! "Why was she here?"
I wondered. "Maybe she knows?"

She came out of the woods and walked up to the feeder.

"Who are you?" I barked. "I'm Dottie the Doe," she answered quickly," and I'm here for some delicious bird seed!"

Dottie was tall.
"Did you knock the birdfeeder down?" I asked.
"Yes, I did. I'm sorry, but I was so hungry! This seed is good for more than just birds, especially when the ground is frozen," she explained.

"Look, I brought my sister Daisy to enjoy the feast!
This time, I will try not to knock the feeder down."
They carefully ate their fill and then headed back
into the woods.

*With the help of my friends, I solved
The Mystery at the Birdfeeder. It was Dottie the Doe.
Now I could finally take a nap.*

The End.

Where the Book Came From

As an avid photographer, I like taking pictures of scenery and wildlife (including my dogs). I was attempting to get some pictures of birds when a surprise photo opportunity arose. A deer brazenly came to the birdfeeder and proceeded to enjoy the birdseed. I managed to capture a picture of the deer, with her tongue in the birdfeeder, through the dining room window! I then got several shots of the deer staring at me through the window, as if to ask why I was interrupting her. Since I have stayed with a film camera, I had to wait for the pictures to be developed. Once I saw the picture of the deer, with her tongue in the birdfeeder, I knew it was the beginning of a book. So I spent the rest of the winter of 2008-2009 taking pictures of birds and thinking about a story line. Purdy, our female English Setter, loves to sit on her dog house roof and observe whatever is happening. She evolved as the star of the book since her dog house was in the background of many of the photographs. After a few rounds of revisions, and a title suggestion by my granddaughter Lora, we had the final copy: "The Mystery at the Birdfeeder." We hope you enjoy the photographs as well as the story.

Wayne and Purdy

The picture that started the book.

P.S. Purdy's brother, Rusty, will be in the next book in the series

Glossary
Cast of birds in order of appearance

Northern Cardinal

The Northern Cardinal is a seed eater. Their beak has sharp edges to crack open the seeds. Black-oil sunflower seeds are a favorite, in addition to safflower seeds. They eat seeds in general, along with insects, fruit, and grain. Cardinals prefer eating closer to the ground or on the ground. Found in Eastern and Southern United States.
Sources 2, 3, 4.

Slate-colored Dark-eyed Junco

The Dark-eyed Junco is mostly a seed-eater. They enjoy seeds of chickweed, buckwheat, lamb's quarters, and sorrel. When the Junco visits the bird feeder it prefers millet to sunflower seeds, leaving them for the cardinal, chickadee and titmouse. The junco also eats insects such as beetles, moths, butterflies, caterpillars, ants, wasps, and flies. Dark-eyed Juncos can be found throughout the continental United States during the winter and in Canada and Alaska in the warm summer months. They can be found year around in the Northeast states, some Western states, and Northern Michigan.
Source 3.

Red Breasted Nuthatch

The Red Breasted Nuthatch prefers to eat insects and similar creatures such as beetles, caterpillars, spiders, ants, and earwigs. When available, they also feed on the spruce bud-worm. In the fall and winter they eat conifer seeds, many of which they hid earlier in the year. When a feeder is available, the nuthatch enjoys peanuts, sunflower seeds, and suet. The Red Breasted Nuthatch is found in Canada and some Western states year around, and in all of the continental United States during the Winter.
Source 3.

Tufted Titmouse

The Tufted Titmouse likes the same food as the Chickadee, seeds, suet, and insects. The bigger the seed, the better, as the Titmouse chooses the largest seed available when at a birdfeeder. Insects eaten include caterpillars, beetles, ants, wasps, stink bugs, and treehoppers in addition to spiders and snails. Nuts, berries, acorns, and beech nuts are not too big to eat. The Tufted Titmouse can be found all along the Eastern United States.
Sources: 3, 4.

White Breasted Nuthatch

The White Breasted Nuthatch eats mainly insects and similar creatures including weevil larvae, wood-boring beetle larvae, beetles, tree hoppers, scale insects, ants, caterpillars, stinkbugs, click beetles, and spiders. Also in their diet are acorns, hawthorn, sunflower seeds, and sometimes corn. At birdfeeders they enjoy sunflower seeds, peanuts, suet, and peanut butter. The White Breasted Nuthatch likes to feed with other birds, as it feels more comfortable. If there are no titmice around, the nuthatch will probably stay away, sensing danger. The White Breasted Nuthatch is found year around in most of the continental United States, Mexico, and parts of Western Canada.
Source 3.

Black-capped Chickadee

The Black-capped Chickadee enjoys black-oil sunflower seeds and safflower seeds but also likes suet. During warmer months insects, spiders, and other animal food make up about 80-90 percent of their diet. In the winter seeds, berries, and plant matter account for more than half of their diet. The Black-capped Chickadee can be found from the Northern United States and Canada and through to the southern portion of Alaska.
Sources: 3, 4.

Red-bellied Woodpecker

The Red-bellied Woodpecker feeds on insects and finds them in the cracks in the bark of trees. Finding a birdfeeder, they enjoy the seeds and will push away other birds, except the more aggressive Blue Jay. The Red-bellied Woodpecker can be found in most areas of the United States, east of the Mississippi River.
Source 3.

Wild Turkey

The Wild Turkey feeds on acorns, nuts, seeds, fruits, insects, buds, fern fronds, and salamanders. It is found in much of the Eastern United States and various parts of the Western States and Mexico.
Source 3.

Bibliography - Sources

1. National Audubon Society Pocket Guide: Familiar Birds of North America – East
Ann H. Whitman, Editor. A Borzoi Book. (Published by Alfred A. Knopf, Inc. 1986. Eleventh Printing 2000)

2. An Audubon Handbook Eastern Birds
John Farrand, Jr. A Chanticleer Press Edition. (McGraw-Hill Book Company 1988)

3. The Cornell Lab of Ornithology website All About Birds
www.allaboutbirds.com
www.allaboutbirds.org/guide/Northern_Cardinal/lifehistory#at_food

4. Bird Source web site. Birding with a Purpose
www.birdsource.org
www.birdsource.org/gbbc/learning/bird-feeding-tips/what-kind-of-bird-food-should-i-use

Acknowledgements

Many people have been an encouragement to me to move forward with this book. Thanks to all of you! I thank Carl Sams for his sage advice, which has been very helpful. Many thanks to David Haslam, my publisher, for the faith he has had in the success of this book and all of the work he has done to make it possible. Thanks are also due to his wife, Cecilia, for her help with the script as the book grew in length. Thanks also to Elena for the great work with the photographs; Monica for her fine edits; and Jennelle for her assistance keeping everyone on time. A big "Thank You" to my wife, Patricia, who helped identify the birds, put up with the camera and tripod in the dining room, and for her review of the text in behalf of young readers. I must also thank my daughter, Stephanie Root (who went to the Center for Creative Studies in Detroit,) for her discriminating review of both pictures and text, to be sure it was worthy of being published. Thanks also to my granddaughter, Lora Root, who came up with the new name for this book after it expanded into the mystery version!

Wayne L. Brillhart
Hartland, Michigan

October, 2009